Dònal Òg in the Forest of the Walking and Talking Trees

Book Three of the Dònal Òg Series

by

Donal McCarthy

Illustrations by Emily Fuhrer

Website: **DonalOgSeries.com**

Joshua Tree Publishing

• Chicago •

Dònal Òg in the Forest of the Walking and Talking Trees

Book Three of the Dònal Òg Series
by Donal McCarthy

Published by
Joshua Tree Publishing
• Chicago •
JoshuaTreePublishing.com

13-Digit ISBN: 978-1-956823-05-9

Credits: All Illustrations by Emily Fuhrer
Website: **DonalOgSeries.com**

Disclaimer:

Printed in the United States of America

Dedication

To my daughters
Cara, Ashling, and Níamh
and my grandaughters
Eden and Aria

Thank You

Emily Fuhrer
Ami on Vancouver Island
John Paul Owles

Dònal Òg in the Forest of the Walking and Talking Trees

The moon shone brightly over the wild bogland, bathing everything in its clear white light, as Dònal Òg looked out from his bedroom window. A mist covered the land as far as the eye could see. Here and there, a lone tree seemed to float above it, but the strangest sight of all was a herd of cows that seemed to have no legs but were still upright.

A fox barked with a lonely sound and was answered from a far-off place by another. Dònal Òg shivered.

Aunt Tess had told him that the foxes pass along messages over long distances for the fairy folk. He wondered what they were saying to each other. Just then, a large bird flew across the moon. It was a gray heron that gave a loud call as it flew off in the direction of the magic forest. A horse in a nearby field whinnied softly and then carried on grazing on the dew-laden grass.

In the next valley, a dog howled at the shining orb and then fell silent. Dònal Òg thought that something strange was happening. Birds and animals seemed to be uneasy out there in the fields. Faintly, he heard the sound of marching feet. *Tramp, tramp, tramp,* it went. *Tramp, tramp, tramp, tramp* over and over and over again. The sound seemed to be approaching the cottage.

A swirl of wind lifted the mist for a moment, and he saw a long column of fairies marching toward him. They marched right past and continued straight toward the fairy fort. For the longest time, he listened as the tiny feet marched past, no longer visible under the mist. He wondered if there was new mischief afoot. Were the fairies preparing to break their agreement with the humans again and go to war with them? He hoped not. Ever since he had upset the fairies and started the trouble between them and the humans, he was afraid that trouble would break out again despite their peace agreements.

Thinking that he would be much better off if he returned to his warm bed, he did just that. Climbing under the blankets and pulling them under his chin, he soon drifted off to sleep. Soon he was dreaming that he was running with his cousins Eden and Aria through fields that were filled with flowers of many different colors. There were buttercups of the brightest yellow and tall foxgloves with pink fingers. The hedgerow was full of yellow gorse, orange montbretia, and purple fuchsia. The crow of the rooster woke him up to a lovely summer day.

He heard Ma working in the kitchen. The call to come and get his breakfast had him leaping out of bed and heading downstairs. Both Aria and Eden were already there. He was glad to see that Ma was ladling out the porridge. Da had bought a new pot so that they no longer had to eat potatoes for every meal.

"Hurry up, lazy bones," said the girls. "Today, we are going to find baby rabbits and catch fish in the river."

Dònal Òg told Ma about what he had seen in the night and how the troop of fairies had marched up to the fort. A frown appeared on Ma's face. What did it mean? More trouble? She hoped not. There was much work to be done about the cottage and in the fields. Every time she had to call a war council with her generals, it took up a lot of her time. They also drank all her tea and ate all her currant cake. Not that she minded, but it would be great if one of them considered bringing a cake or two along with them. She herself would never go to any of their houses without taking a cake along. *It takes all sorts*, she thought.

Just then, there was a squeaking sound from near the front door. Her hair stood straight up on her head, and sweat broke out on her forehead. She was just about to throw the kettle of boiling water at the rat when she realized that it was the weasel.

Sweet Jesus! she thought. *This is all I need right at this minute!*

"Good morning, Mistress," the weasel was saying, but all Ma could hear was *squeak, squeak, squeak!* Eden ran to the weasel and picked him up to stroke him. Aria ran to call Aunt Tess, who understood weasel speak. Soon she was sitting at the table with a pot of tea in front of her and looking around to see where the cake was. When none was forthcoming, she asked what all the fuss was about.

Eden brought the weasel to her, and they started conversing. When it was over, the weasel ran back to the girls, and Aunt Tess and Ma sat talking. Aunt Tess told Ma that the weasel had come on behalf of Queen Niamh to inform them that festivities were being held at the fort for the inauguration of the new king and queen and that she hoped the music wouldn't cause them any disturbance.

As with humans, the fairies also had their rituals to celebrate the crowning of their royals. Ma was so pleased to find out that it wasn't more trouble that she soon had a large plate of cake in front of them.

"Goodness me! It looks like I forgot to offer you some," she said to Aunt Tess.

Leaving Ma and Aunt Tess to themselves, the children set off on their rabbit hunt.

Along the hedgerows, they crept silently. Soon they saw the rabbits in the meadow. The older ones nibbled furiously at the grass while the younger ones raced back and forth, jumping over each other and then racing around again. Soon a rabbit sentry spotted the children. Stamping his back feet, he sent out the alarm signal. Within a split second, the meadow was empty. The rabbits, young and old, had sped back to their burrows and disappeared underground.

Pffff! Just like that, the meadow looked like it had never seen a rabbit.

Waiting for a little while, they decided to lie in the meadow and count how many birds flew past. Eden saw a blackbird while Aria a thrush. Dònal Òg saw a hen, but they wouldn't let him count that.

Girls are so bossy! he thought. Then he saw a cock pheasant, which made them jealous. He thought it should count as ten birds as it was the biggest and most beautiful bird they had seen.

A long discussion followed as Aria thought that wasn't fair as it was so big it was impossible not to see it. She had just been about to shout it out, but he was faster. Dònal Òg was having none of it! He often heard Da say that women could start a fight in an empty room. Now for the first time, he was beginning to understand what Da meant. It didn't matter what you said; they found a way to argue about it. So Dònal Òg started on the long road of trying to understand females.

They decided to go to the river and try to catch some fish. Maybe if they caught a big one, they could make a fire and cook it for lunch. Dònal Òg had been reading about a special salmon that swam in the rivers of Ireland. Anyone catching it and eating it would become very wise and clever.

Eden thought her mom had already given them a lot of that fish to eat! For the next hour, they stood in the cool water, bending over and searching among the reeds and rocks. They saw many small sprats, frogs, and tadpoles but no fish big enough to make a meal.

A herd of cows stood under the trees, swishing their tails to drive away the flies that were pestering them. The worst one was the gadfly. Its bite was so sharp that it caused them pain. So they stood head to tail—each one's tail kept the flies off the other one's face—and wondered what the strange two-legged creatures that owned them were doing. They weren't eating, they weren't drinking, and they were making a lot of noise and disturbing their peace. Then they ignored them.

Soon the children got bored with the fishing and decided to run home and get something to eat. Ma was in the kitchen, making a big plate of sliced homemade bread with lots of butter and delicious strawberry jam for them. They ate it while drinking big mugs of sweet tea. With tummies soon full, they were ready for some adventure.

"Take us to see the magic forest and the talking trees," said Aria. "You promised that you would!"

Dònal Òg regretted ever having spoken about the place. He was very scared of it. Ma had forbidden him to enter the forest unless Da was with him. "Strange things happened there," she said as she blessed herself and threw salt over her right shoulder. Now with his two cousins staring at him, he didn't know how to not go. He didn't want to look like a coward in front of them. After all, everyone knew that he was a big strong, brave hero. Hadn't he single-handedly outsmarted the fairy king?

Okay, so he had a little help from a few older women, but he was the hero! Thinking furiously wasn't helping, so he resigned himself to going. Filling their pockets with salt while Ma wasn't looking, they called out that they were going out to play. Ma warned them to take care and be back in time for dinner.

Off they ran and soon found themselves on a long winding dirt track leading to the forest. Ferns and furze bush grew side by side in a blaze of green and yellow.

"This looks just like what I always thought a path to a magic forest should look like," said Aria. Eden agreed while Dònal Òg said nothing. He was too busy looking around for the first signs of trouble. Ma always said, "Never trouble trouble until trouble troubles you." He should have listened to her, he thought.

He peered closely through the bush, and his heart nearly stopped when he saw a giant's face staring right at them.

With deep-set eyes, a hooked nose, a huge mouth, and a pointy chin, it seemed to be screaming silently at them. "Keep out! Run away whilst you still can!" it seemed to be saying.

Behind it, on a log, he saw two dogs staring off into eternity and barking silently at whatever they were looking at. The knees of Dònal Òg started shaking. He broke into a sweat and couldn't move. He knew that he was looking at trolls that had been put under a spell and frozen in time by the fairies. Further in, he saw the troll's wife, also staring off into space, with a wild growth of greenery where her hair should be. She wasn't looking her best.

"What's wrong?" asked Aria. "Let's keep going!"

With a shaking finger, Dònal Òg pointed toward the bush. "Look!" he squeaked. "Trolls!"

Eden and Aria peered closely and laughed at him. "Those are tree stumps with moss growing on them," Eden said. "Let's go!"

Dònal Òg knew better but felt that he couldn't show fear in front of two girls. They went deeper into the forest, and the path wound up and down and around fallen trees. Every now and then, they passed a dead tree that was still standing. It was full of holes up and down the trunk. That had to be the homes of the wood elves that guarded the entrance to the forest. The children's passage was not unnoticed. Squirrels sitting quietly on tree stumps and branches passed the word along to the ravens that sat higher up on the trees. They, in turn, called it out over the woodland that strangers were intruding. "Beware! Beware! Beware!" they called so that all the inhabitants were informed.

The deer stood silently with their young close to them and stared as the children passed by, totally unaware that they were being watched so closely.

Soon they came to the banks of the Doughlasha, the same stream that flowed past their home. Here in the quiet of the forest, it flowed happily along, singing to itself of all the wonders that it had seen so far.

Aria wanted to drink some water as she was feeling thirsty. As she bent down to cup a handful, Dònal Òg shouted out, "Don't! This water belongs to the fairies. As long as the stream flows through the woods, anyone drinking from it becomes bewitched!"

Jumping back, they all failed to see or hear the sigh of disappointment from the nearby bushes. Had they looked carefully, they would have seen a dozen wood elves staring back at them. The wood elves weren't bad creatures; they liked to dance with human children to the music from their flutes. The problem was that if the children hadn't drunk the water before they saw them, they would run away in fright. It was better that they drank and became bewitched; then, they were happy to dance all night long.

Unaware of any of this, the children moved back into the forest. Everywhere they looked, they could see dead trees covered with moss that hung off them like garments. Here was a mother and her three children heading for church. Just a little behind was father hurrying to catch up. He had to make sure that the goat couldn't get into the cabbage before he left. They were waving to each other when the spell had hit them. Now they reached out to each other for eternity.

Dònal Òg could see it all clearly in his mind's eye. Over there were a group of boys frozen on the spot as they raced down the track. A little closer was what looked like an older woman bending over to straighten her stocking. He wondered what had caused all this to happen. It all looked as if it had happened before anyone could react. Everything looked so calm and peaceful. It was hard to imagine it happening at all. He didn't speak his thoughts to Eden and Aria; they already thought he was a scaredy-cat from earlier.

They came to a clearing where stood the biggest tree that they had ever seen; it went straight up to the sky. Aria thought it was even higher than the clouds. Eden said it was wider than the cottage. They sat beneath its spreading branches; it gave beautiful shade from the hot sun. Sitting quietly, they soon saw and heard all the creatures that lived in the sprawling canopy and on the trunk of the tree itself.

Ants marched in single file up the trunk to some distant destination. A centipede undulated on a separate journey. Woodpeckers kept an eye on them both, no doubt planning an ambush somewhere along the route. Squirrels raced around and through the branches. Birds of many different kinds perched among the leaves—either resting, preening, or singing a song of courtship. Unmindful of it all, the tree slumbered on.

Soon the children could feel their eyes closing. The drone of the bees' wings and the birdsong were making them sleepy. Dònal Òg knew that they mustn't fall asleep, not here in the magic forest. Try as hard as he could, he couldn't stop it. Soon they were sound asleep. As they slept, the animals crept closer to see the children. The red deer brought a fawn and stood silently looking on. The fox was there, as well as the badger with its cub. The rabbit, weasel, and ferret gathered around. The otter left the stream, and the hedgehog the undergrowth. The trout thought of joining them, but the exercise left him gasping for breath, so he flopped back into the water.

The parents explained the human children to their young. "They can be very kind," one of them said, "but also very cruel."

"They shoot stones at us with their catapults that can hurt us badly or kill us. They also steal our eggs and babies from our nests," said the bird.

"They lay wire snares that can tighten around our neck and choke us to death or catch our legs so that we can't move. Then we lie in agony for days until we starve to death or get eaten by another animal," said the rabbit as he looked meaningfully at the fox.

"They dig out our home," said the fox. "And then they chase us with their dogs."

"And all because we lack opposable thumbs," said the badger to the otter, who looked at him and thought, *Now that's an odd fellow*, before inching away from him discreetly.

They all melted back into the forest, and none but the forest creatures ever knew that they had ever been there. A loud sneeze startled the children out of their sleep.

"Bless you," said Eden.

"Thank you," said a deep voice.

Looking all around, the children couldn't see anyone. Just then, another louder sneeze seemed to come from the tree they were sitting under.

"Come out, whoever you are," said Eden crossly. "It's rude to hide and startle people."

"Forgive my rudeness," said the deep voice, "but the presence of humans always makes me sneeze."

They looked at each other in amazement. Was it possible that someone was hiding up among the branches of the tree?

"Come down and let us see you!" Aria demanded.

"I can't come down from myself," said the voice. "You are standing right next to me beneath my branches. Surely you must be able to see me!"

"Do you mean that you are a talking tree?" asked both girls at the same time.

"Yes," it replied. "My name is Dharaig. Because you slept peacefully in my shade, I must reveal myself to you and protect you from anyone and anything that might want to harm you in this forest."

"That is very kind of you," said Aria.

"We are honored to meet you. You must be the king of all trees," said Eden. "I would like to introduce ourselves to you. I am Eden, and this is my sister Aria. This is our cousin Dònal Òg."

"I know who he is," said Dharaig. "Word of his doings is known to all of us here. How he has set fire to some of our cousins whom he burns to heat his food and keep his cottage warm. How he tricked the old fairy king. Yes! We know you, Dònal Òg! As long as you behave yourself here in my forest, you are welcome and under my protection. Step out of line and cause any pain to any of the trees or creatures living here, and you shall be turned into a petrified creature like you saw on your way here today."

Both girls looked at Dònal Òg with big eyes. "You were right," Aria said. "Those were people!"

"Why were they turned into petrified creatures?" asked Eden. "What did they do?"

"They came into our beautiful forest home many eons ago," said Dharaig. "At first, they were good and kind, and we welcomed them. We gave them shade from the hot sun and from the cold rain. The animals showed them where to find food and water. The birds showed them which berries were safe to eat and which were not. Then they started cutting down all our sisters and brothers to build their shelters and light their fires. Then they started trapping and killing the animals and birds that had been kind to them.

Soon, our forest home was filled with pain and despair. Our rivers turned brown and muddy and dried up. Our very soil cried out in pain as they burned all the growth so that they could plant their own foreign crops—crops that brought sickness and disease to our home. A meeting was called between the elders of all the various tree tribes to find a solution to the problem. After much discussion, it was decided to cast a spell on all the humans entering or living in the forest. They were to be petrified and turned into wood as a warning to all others who would enter and harm the forest.

"The spell would last as long as humans kept hurting forests everywhere. The only exception was to be children entering the forest for the first time. If they caused any damage, they were to be given a warning by the wood elves. If they didn't listen, they would be chased from the woods by trolls. If that didn't scare them enough and they came back again, they would be turned into petrified stumps like all the others."

All this talk of being turned into a stump was making Dònal Òg very nervous. "It's getting quite late," he said. "Ma will be getting worried. We better be heading off home."

"Yes, it is!" said Dharaig. "It's too late now for you to get to the edge of the woods before darkness falls. If you are not out of here by then, all sorts of trouble can befall you. Trolls and ogres roam around after dark ready to capture anyone found trespassing. They bewitch them and turn them into mindless creatures who have to do their bidding forever and ever."

"If that happens to us," said Dònal Òg, "Ma will kill me."

"Climb into my branches," said Dharaig, "and I will take you to the edge of the forest and safety."

"Your branches are too high off the ground," said Eden as she looked up into the tree. "We will never be able to climb up to them."

Dharaig lowered the tip of one of the branches, and they scrambled into it. Soon they were sitting high above the other trees. They could see to the far edge of the forest. They could see the light in the cottage where they knew the adults would be waiting anxiously.

Slowly Dharaig lifted his roots out of the earth. So deep did they go that it seemed to take forever. Slowly they inched forward with many a "Pardon me!" and even more sorries. As he stood on his brethren, Dharaig made painful progress. The children could see the torches as the adults searched the fields and riverbanks as the night wore on. The sun was about to climb over the horizon as they finally reached the edge of the forest.

Dharaig lowered his branch once more to the ground to allow the children to scramble down.

"Thank you so much for being so kind and helping us," Eden said. "From this day on, we will see trees in a different light and will never again do anything to cause pain or suffering to one or allow anyone else to do it either."

"Before we leave you," said Dònal Òg, "I need to ask you a question."

"Feel free!" said Dharaig.

"Does this mean we can no longer burn the firewood to heat our homes and food?" asked Dònal Òg.

"Not at all!" said Dharaig. "As long as the wood is dead, it feels nothing. By burning it, you release its spirit back into the soil much faster as ash than if it has to rot."

Dònal Òg was very relieved. The thought of having to forage in the hedgerows again had him in a cold sweat.

"We are going to be in big trouble with everyone," said Eden. "They have been searching for us all night long and are very worried. They will think that the fairies stole us away."

"Don't worry," said Dharaig. "Leave it to me." With that, he blew a soft breeze toward the far-off humans. It carried a magic spell with it. They all returned to their homes and forgot that they had been worried and looking for the children. As Dharaig started his journey back to the forest, the creatures living on him complained among themselves.

"What a night!" said a bird. "We didn't get a moment's sleep with all the talking and squealing."

"Tell us about it," said one of the squirrels. "We kept slipping off every time he jolted his roots on something."

The owl said nothing—he had been out hunting and had just now returned and was ready for sleep. When the adults awoke a little later, feeling refreshed and happy, they woke the children up for breakfast.

"Get up, sleepyheads," Ma said. "We all seem to have overslept today."

The children looked at each other and said nothing. It had been a close call and a wonderful adventure. Aria wanted to tell Ma about it, but Dònal Òg and Eden swore her to secrecy. If they told Ma, then they would be grounded and not allowed any more adventures. Dònal Òg still wanted to show them the shaking bog where he saw a wild duck land one day. One minute it was there; the next, it had disappeared. *Kazaam!* It was gone, just like that! Two minutes later, three feathers and an egg floated to the top, nothing else.

But that's a story for another day!

The End.

READ THE DÒNAL ÒG SERIES

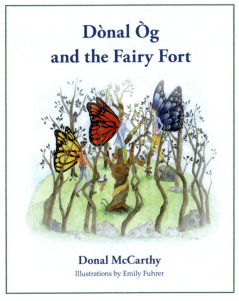

Dònal Òg and the Fairy Fort

Donal McCarthy

Illustrations by Emily Fuhrer

BOOK ONE

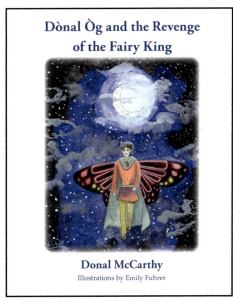

Dònal Òg and the Revenge of the Fairy King

Donal McCarthy

Illustrations by Emily Fuhrer

BOOK TWO

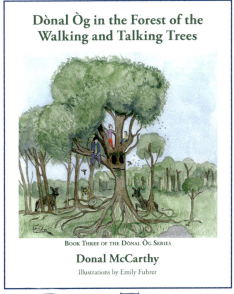

Dònal Òg in the Forest of the Walking and Talking Trees

BOOK THREE OF THE DÒNAL ÒG SERIES

Donal McCarthy

Illustrations by Emily Fuhrer

BOOK THREE

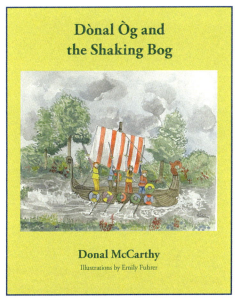

Dònal Òg and the Shaking Bog

Donal McCarthy

Illustrations by Emily Fuhrer

BOOK FOUR

Website: **DonalOgSeries.com**

Manufactured by Amazon.ca
Bolton, ON

25562389R00021